Madeline
the Cookie
Fairy

Special thanks to Rachel Elliot

ISBN 978-0-545-60535-9

Previously published as Sweet Fairies #5: *Madeleine the Cookie Fairy* by Orchard U.K. in 2013.

All rights reserved. Published by Scholastic Inc., 557 Broadway, New York, NY 10012, by arrangement with Rainbow Magic Limited.

12 11 10 9 8 7 6 5 4 3 2 1   14 15 16 17 18 19/0

Printed in the U.S.A.   40

This edition first printing, March 2014

Madeline

the Cookie

Fairy

by Daisy Meadows

SCHOLASTIC INC.

The Fairyland Palace

Candy Land

Goblins' ice cream truck

Market booth

Charlie's ice cream truck

Kirsty's House

Wetherbury Village

I have a plan to make a mess
And cause the fairies much distress.
I'm going to take their charms away
And make my dreams come true today!

I'll build a castle made of sweets,
And ruin the fairies' silly treats.
I just don't care how much they whine,
Their cakes and candies will be mine!

Contents

In the Candy Land Cafeteria

The yellow walls of the Candy Land
factory gleamed in the midday sun, and
the colorful flags on its roof waved in the
spring breeze. In the factory cafeteria,
Rachel Walker and Kirsty Tate were
finishing their sandwiches and chatting
with Kirsty's aunt Helen.

"You're so lucky to work here," Rachel said. "It's my dream job!"

"You wouldn't say that if you saw all the paperwork I have to do," replied Aunt Helen with a laugh.

"Yes, but you get to taste all the new candy," said Kirsty with a giggle. "That sounds like the best job in the world!"

Aunt Helen laughed and glanced up at the clock on the wall.

"It *does* mean I was able to organize a tour of the factory for my favorite niece and her best friend!" she said with a smile. "Have you enjoyed the tour so far?"

Tomorrow was Kirsty's birthday, and this special day at Candy Land was an early birthday present. Since Rachel was staying with Kirsty over spring break, she had gotten to come along, too. Lucky her!

"It's been amazing!" said Rachel. "The chocolate department was really cool."

"Yes, thank you for the tickets, Aunt Helen," said Kirsty. "Today is one of the best birthday presents I've ever had!"

"It's not over yet," said Aunt Helen with a grin. "You'll be spending this afternoon with me in the cookie department. But first, I have another little treat for you. Wait here! I'll be right back."

She winked at them and headed to the cafeteria counter. Rachel and Kirsty looked at each other with shining eyes.

"I don't know how this day could get any better!" said Rachel. "Isn't this just perfect?"

She waved her arm around at the cafeteria. Everything at Candy Land looked like sweet treats, so the tables were  huge cakes and the chairs were enormous cookies.

"Look," whispered Kirsty, nudging her best friend. "That boy has a Sticky Toffee Galore. My favorite!"

Rachel glanced at the boy, who was sitting at the next table.

"It looks yummy," she said. "I'm so glad that chocolate tastes good again."

The girls were right in the middle of an exciting fairy adventure! Jack Frost had stolen the Sugar and Spice Fairies' magic charms, which they used to make sure that treats in both Fairyland and the human world were delicious. He wanted to build a giant Candy Castle! Even worse, he was trying to ruin Treat Day in Fairyland. Usually, Queen Titania and King Oberon gave each fairy a special basket of sweet treats as a thank you for all their hard work. But there wouldn't be any treats this year—unless Kirsty and Rachel could help all seven Sugar and Spice Fairies get their charms back!

That morning, Jack Frost and his

greedy goblins had caused a chocolate disaster at Candy Land. Luckily, Kirsty and Rachel had been able to help the fairies fix everything!

"I hope the goblins won't cause any trouble this afternoon," said Kirsty. "But there are still three more  magic charms to find, so we have to keep an eye out for them."

Jack Frost had given the charms to his goblins for safekeeping, and ordered them to bring all the yummy treats from the human world to his Candy Castle.

"We've already helped four of the Sugar and Spice Fairies get their magic charms back," said Rachel with a gleam in her eye. "I just hope that we can find the others before it's too late!"

Cookie Crisis

"Aunt Helen is coming back," said Kirsty. "We'll have to finish talking about the goblins later."

Aunt Helen was carrying a cream-colored bag with swirly blue writing on the side.

Cookie Creations
Delicious cookies made especially for you!

Kirsty and Rachel looked at each other in concern.

"Jack Frost still has Madeline the Cookie Fairy's magic charm," whispered Rachel. "I have a feeling that these cookies might not be as delicious as they're supposed to be. . . ."

"These are for you, girls," said Aunt Helen, taking two cookies from the bag. "I asked for your names to be written on them, but I don't think the person behind the counter was listening."

The girls thanked her and took the cookies. They were covered with messy

splotches of icing in ugly colors. Rachel
and Kirsty each took a small bite . . .
and then exchanged surprised smiles.

"Wow!" said
Kirsty. "This
tastes so good!"

"Mine, too," said
Rachel, taking
another bite.
"Delicious!"

"Glad you like them!" said Aunt Helen
with a beaming smile. "Now, it's time
for us to go to the cookie department.
I'm hoping that you can help me with
my work."

The girls finished their cookies and
followed Aunt Helen through the
cafeteria.

"Look," said Rachel, pointing to one

corner of the cafeteria. "That's the Cookie Creations counter."

"And there's the cookie kitchen, behind it," Kirsty added.

"That's where they make the cookies and decorate them to order," Aunt Helen explained.

"*Mmm*, I can smell the cookies baking!" said Rachel, sniffing the air in delight.

As the girls followed Aunt Helen through the cafeteria to the cookie department, Kirsty frowned thoughtfully.

"I don't understand how the Cookie Creations cookies can taste so delicious. Jack Frost has the magic cookie charm," she whispered to Rachel.

"Maybe Madeline managed to find it in Fairyland," said Rachel.

Just then, Aunt Helen stopped outside a door marked COOKIE DESIGN ROOM. She took two white aprons from pegs on the wall and handed them to the girls.

"Every cookie designer has to wear an apron," she said, her eyes twinkling.

When the girls walked through the door, a wonderful aroma filled the air. Men and women in green aprons were hurrying around, and pictures of all kinds of cookies decorated the walls.

"Mmm," said Rachel, sniffing the air. "I can smell cinnamon and chocolate and roasting nuts and cookie dough!"

"I want to show you some sketches of new cookies I've designed," said Aunt Helen, leading them to a desk in one corner of the room.

She laid some sheets of paper out on the desk. Each sheet showed a beautiful drawing of a cookie, with tiny arrows pointing to the things that made that cookie special.

"These are Jammy Hearts," said Aunt Helen, pointing to the first design.

"They're heart-shaped sandwich cookies filled with jam."

"I like the look of these," said Rachel, pointing to a cookie with a happy face made out of chocolate chips.

"Those are called Chocolate Smiles," Aunt Helen told her.

"This picture's making my mouth water," said Kirsty, looking at a design for oatmeal raisin cookies.

"Yes, those are Oaty Surprises," said Aunt Helen. "They're my favorites, too."

"If these taste half as good as the ones we had from Cookie Creations, they'll be great!" said Rachel.

"Thanks, girls," said Aunt Helen. "It's good to hear that people will like them!"

Just then, the door flew open. A man

who worked
in the
factory
hurried in,
carrying a
tray of
cookies. He
looked very
upset.

"Helen, we
have a big problem," he said, holding out
the tray. "All of these cookies are
ruined—look! I don't know what's
wrong. There's no jam in the Jammy
Hearts, the Chocolate Smiles are missing
the chocolate chip faces, and the Oaty
Surprises don't have any raisins!"

Aunt Helen frowned.

"Maybe it's because they're new," she said. "We must have made a mistake with the cookie machine settings."

The factory worker shook his head.

"But even the traditional gingerbread cookies are turning out wrong. They all have enormous feet and pointy ears. We've been making those for ages, so it can't be the settings."

Rachel looked at the gingerbread cookie on the tray and nudged Kirsty.

"That gingerbread man looks more like a gingerbread *goblin* to me," she whispered. Her eyes widened. "Kirsty, I think the goblins must be right here in the cookie department!"

Kitchen Surprise

Aunt Helen looked worried.

"Girls, do you mind waiting here while I go and check the cookie machine?" she asked. "While I'm gone, you can look through my cookie cutters and pick out the ones you like best."

She handed the girls a box that was filled with cookie cutters of every shape and size. Then she hurried off with the factory worker.

"There have been so many problems at Candy Land lately," Rachel and Kirsty heard her say. "I can't understand it."

The girls looked at each other. They knew exactly why everything was going wrong!

"Jack Frost is terrible," said Kirsty. "Aunt Helen has been so nice to us. It's really unfair that she should have to worry about all this."

"If we can help all the Sugar and Spice Fairies, that will help your aunt Helen, too," said Rachel.

"Yes," Kirsty agreed. "We just have to wait for our chance to find the next magic charm."

They started to look through the box.

"There must be every cookie cutter ever made here!" said Rachel with a laugh. "Stars . . . butterflies . . . flowers . . . even gingerbread men and women!"

"Oh, look at this one!" exclaimed Kirsty, picking up a castle-shaped cookie cutter. "It looks just like the king and queen's palace in Fairyland!"

"It's really pretty," said Rachel. "I wonder if there are any others like that in here."

She peered into the bottom of the box, and gave a little squeal of excitement.

"Kirsty, look!" she said. "That cookie cutter in the corner is glowing!"

"It's the shape of a fairy!" said Kirsty. "Oh, Rachel, do you think it could be . . . ?"

Rachel picked it up, and the glow grew brighter. A tiny puff of fairy dust sparkled around the edges of the cookie cutter, and then Madeline the Cookie Fairy fluttered up through the middle!

"Hello, Madeline!" said the girls in delight.

The little fairy was so happy to see them that she did a backward somersault in the air. She was wearing purple pants covered in colorful stars, and  her cheeks were pink with excitement.

"Hello, Rachel! Hello, Kirsty!" she said, speaking very quickly. "I'm so glad I found you! The goblins are somewhere here at Candy Land with my magic charm."

"We think the goblins are here, too," said Rachel. "Something's wrong with the cookie machine."

"The only cookies that haven't been ruined are the ones we got from Cookie Creations," Kirsty added. "They were delicious."

"Oh!" said Rachel, putting her hand to her mouth and opening her eyes wide. "Of course! Madeline, I think your charm must be 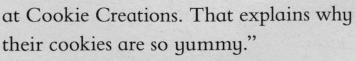 at Cookie Creations. That explains why their cookies are so yummy."

"If I don't get my charm back soon, all

cookies
everywhere
will be ruined,"
said Madeline,
tucking her
blonde hair
behind her ears.

"I have to find those goblins! Girls, will
you help me?"

"Of course we will," said Kirsty and
Rachel together.

"We should go and search the Cookie
Creations kitchen," Rachel added. "Do
you think we have time to go now?"

Kirsty glanced around to see if anyone
was looking. All of the cookie designers
were hard at work. But just then, the
door opened. Aunt Helen was coming
back!

"Quick!" Kirsty whispered to
Madeline. "Hide in my apron pocket!"

Madeline swooped into the pocket of
Kirsty's apron just as Aunt Helen walked
over. She was carrying a tray piled high
with ruined cookies.

"Did you fix the machine?" asked
Rachel.

"Not yet," said Aunt Helen with a sigh.
"The engineers are working on it now.
I brought the ruined cookies back here,

because even though we can't sell them, it would be a shame to waste them. They're not burned, just funny shapes with some missing ingredients. I thought they could be used at Cookie Creations, instead. We could decorate them to order and sell them at a discount."

"Could we take the trays to Cookie Creations for you?" Kirsty offered right away.

Aunt Helen gave her a grateful smile. "That's really sweet of you, Kirsty," she said. "It would help me a lot. These machine problems mean that I have a ton of extra work to do!"

She handed the tray to Kirsty.

"Is it all right if we look around the Cookie Creations kitchen while we're there?" Rachel asked.

"Of course," said Aunt Helen. "Take as much time as you want, and tell the baker that I said it was OK."

The girls hurried out of the cookie design room and back down the hallway toward the cafeteria. Lunchtime was over, so the room was almost empty. There was just one group of people in green factory uniforms sitting at a very messy table. They were making so much noise that they didn't even notice Kirsty and Rachel hurry past to the Cookie Creations counter.

The cookie baker was standing at the

counter, decorating cookies. His bright
green apron was smeared with chocolate
and jam, and there were puffs of
powdered sugar in the air around him.
He was wearing a tall chef's hat, which
was much too big for him. All that the
girls could see of his face was . . . a long,
green nose!

Rachel gasped and clutched Kirsty's
arm. "He's a goblin!" she exclaimed.

Fairies in the Factory

Kirsty handed the cookie tray to the goblin baker.

"My aunt Helen sent these," she said, pretending that she didn't know he was a goblin. "The cookie machine is broken, so she'd like you to sell these ruined cookies at a discount."

The goblin curled his lip. "I don't want your ruined cookies!" he squawked.

But then he noticed the gingerbread men with big feet and pointy ears. He snatched one eagerly from the tray, grabbed some bright green icing, and started to decorate it.

"Come on," whispered Rachel. "He's not watching. If Madeline turns us into fairies, we can search for her cookie charm while he's busy."

Kirsty and Rachel ducked down
behind the display counter, and
Madeline popped out of Kirsty's apron
pocket. With a wave of her wand, she
sent a puff of cookie-scented fairy dust
over the girls! They instantly shrank to
fairy-size, and beautiful wings unfurled
from their shoulders in shimmering
rainbow colors.

"I love being
a fairy!" said
Rachel with
a giggle. She
did a somersault
in the air and
swooped
underneath Kirsty.

"Me, too,"
said Kirsty, smiling

at her best friend. "But right now we have to find that cookie charm—and time's running out!"

Before they could decide where to start the search, the noisy group from the lunch table dashed up to the Cookie Creations counter.

"Hide!" whispered Madeline. "Quick, up here!"

She led the girls to the Cookie Creations sign above the counter. They all perched on top of it. From there, they could see the heads of the noisy factory workers. They were all wearing green hats and

bumping into one another, trying to get close to the counter.

"Those factory workers have such enormous feet that I can see them from here," Kirsty whispered.

"I bet they're goblins, too," said Rachel. "Listen to the way they're screeching!"

"More cookies!" the goblins were
shouting. "More cookies NOW!"

"You've had enough," replied the
goblin baker with a frown. "The cookies
are supposed to be for Jack Frost's Candy
Castle, remember? Look what I made to
hang up on the castle walls."

He held up three
cookies. He had
decorated them
as pictures for
Jack Frost to
display in the
castle.

"Show-off!"
sneered the other
goblins, sticking out their
tongues.

"I don't care what you say," shouted the goblin baker, sticking out his tongue, too. "I'm going to make a goblin cookie to hang up in Jack Frost's throne room. He'll be so happy with it that he'll make me your boss!"

The other goblins started making more faces at the baker.

"I'll tell him what you've been doing!" roared the baker.

"You're always telling on us!" one of them complained. "Tattletale!"

He put his thumb to his nose and wiggled his fingers.

"Go away!" the baker shouted. "I want to finish my cookie picture!"

The other goblins stomped away, muttering to one another, and the baker gazed down at the gingerbread goblin.

"I need some chocolate chips for the face," the girls heard him say to himself. He hurried into the cookie kitchen.

"Let's follow him," said Kirsty. "He's making the delicious cookies, so I bet he has the charm."

The girls and Madeline quietly
fluttered after him, keeping high above
his head so he wouldn't spot them. The
sweet-smelling kitchen was warm. There
were a few trays of gingerbread goblins
cooling on the counter. Rachel, Kirsty,
and Madeline watched the baker scurry
over to the pantry. He pulled a bunch of
keys from his pants pocket.

"Girls!" said Madeline with a squeak
of excitement. "Look!"

Among the keys, they could see a small
chocolate-chip cookie charm! It was
glowing.

"That's my magic charm," said
Madeline. "But how are we going to get
it back?"

A Green Transformation

The goblin baker used his keys to open the pantry, and stepped inside. It was a small room, with just enough space for one person to stand inside. The walls were lined with shelves, and the girls spotted giant jars of jam, bags of chocolate chips, and big boxes of raisins.

"Those are all ingredients that are missing from the Candy Land cookies," Kirsty whispered. "That greedy goblin must have taken them all!"

The baker heaved a huge bag of chocolate chips onto his back.

"Jack Frost will really like the gingerbread goblin," he said aloud, chuckling. "Then he'll see that I'm better than all those other silly goblins. I know! I'll make a gingerbread Jack Frost to go with it. He'll love that!"

"I have an idea," said Rachel.

"Madeline, can you make it seem like
the gingerbread goblins are singing?
Maybe we can distract the baker long
enough to get the charm back."

While the baker had his back turned to
lock the pantry, the girls flew over to the
cookie cooling trays. They each picked
up a gingerbread goblin and hid behind
it, while Madeline hovered high above
them, out of sight.

When the goblin turned around with
the bag of chocolate
chips, Rachel
and Kirsty
started to
wiggle the
gingerbread
goblins back and
forth. It looked like
they were dancing! Madeline used her
magic to make it sound like the
gingerbread men were singing, too:

"Jack Frost takes everything sweet,
He's the greediest man you'll ever meet.
So won't you please hold out your arm,
And give us the magic cookie charm?"

The goblin dropped the bag, and his

mouth fell open. He stared at the gingerbread goblins, jingling the key ring in his hand.

"Get ready," Kirsty whispered. "We'll have to fly over there as fast as we can and take the charm."

But then the goblin shook his head and laughed. "I've made so many cookies that I'm imagining they can sing and dance!" he said with a cackle.

The girls would have tried again, but at that moment the door to the kitchen burst open! The noisy goblins poured into the room, yelling for more cookies. One of them grabbed the gingerbread goblin that the baker had decorated and bit its legs off. Kirsty and Rachel quickly flew back up to join Madeline.

"It's hopeless," said Madeline, tears filling her eyes. "I'll never get my charm back."

"Of course you will," said Kirsty in a

firm voice. "I have another plan, and I'm pretty sure it'll work. We just have to be brave. Madeline, I want you to disguise me and Rachel as goblins."

Madeline's hand flew to her mouth.

"Please be careful," she said. "If they realize you're tricking them, they might capture you and take you to the Ice Castle as prisoners."

"We have to do everything we can to get your charm back," said Rachel. "Don't worry, Madeline. We're more than a match for those goblins!"

The girls fluttered to the far corner of

the kitchen, and Madeline waved her wand. They felt themselves growing taller, and their noses and ears became long and pointy. They looked at each other and grinned.

"You're all green!" said Rachel with a giggle.

"So are you!" Kirsty replied. "And your hair is gone."

"I'm glad we don't have to stay like this forever," said Rachel, taking a deep breath. "Come on, let's join the goblins. Don't forget to make your voice sound all screechy!"

Greedy Goblins

The girls elbowed their way past the other goblins, who were all bugging the baker.

"I have to make the cookies for the Candy Castle," he shouted. "Leave me alone!"

"Just one more cookie each!" Kirsty yelled above the squeals of the other goblins. "Then we'll leave you alone!"

"Yes, just one more!" said the other goblins. They always liked when someone took charge and told them what to do. "Then we'll go away."

The baker goblin clapped his hands over his ears to drown out the noise.

"All right!" he hollered. "All right, one more each! Then you have to leave me alone!"

The goblins eagerly started to call out their orders.

"I want sprinkles on mine!"

"Jelly beans!"

"Green icing!"

"I want raisins on mine," said Rachel, remembering which ingredients were locked in the pantry.

"I want jam," added Kirsty.

There was a deafening roar as everyone called out their favorite ingredients. The baker slapped his forehead with his hand.

"Stop, all of you!" he roared. "I can't hear myself think!"

"I'll help," said Rachel in a gruff squawk. "I'll go get all the ingredients for you."

The baker goblin nodded gratefully. He pulled the keys from his pocket and threw them to Rachel.

"Got it!" Rachel exclaimed, unhooking the magic cookie charm.

She and Kirsty ran to the back of the kitchen, and Madeline swooped down to join them.

"What are you doing?" cried the baker in shock. He still thought that the girls were goblins!

"I'm returning this charm to its rightful owner," Rachel replied. She handed the cookie charm to Madeline, and it glowed even more brightly as it shrank to fairy-size.

"TRAITORS!" cried the goblins.

"No, they're HUMANS!" said
Madeline in triumph.

She returned Rachel and Kirsty to
their normal forms, and the goblins
suddenly got very quiet.

"Jack Frost is going to be furious if we
go back without any cookies," said the
baker in a small voice. "What are we
going to do?"

They all hung their heads and stared miserably at their big feet. Madeline felt sorry for them! She waved her wand, and a ribbon of fairy dust looped around the goblins, touching each of them on the hand. Suddenly, every goblin found that he was holding a special cookie. There was a new gingerbread goblin for the baker and a gingerbread Jack Frost. It was decorated with blue and white icing, and it was so lifelike that the baker looked a little bit scared of it!

"When you get home, tell Jack Frost to stop being so greedy," said Kirsty.

"It's not fair to everyone else who likes cookies," Rachel added. "Jack Frost should learn to share!"

Madeline gave a little twirl in the air.

"I'll take the goblins home," she said. "And I'll make sure they don't cause any more mischief on the way!"

"Good-bye!" said Kirsty. "Tell the other Sugar and Spice Fairies that we're here whenever they need us!"

"Good-bye, Madeline!" called Rachel.

Madeline waved and smiled. Then her wand sparkled and she and the goblins disappeared back to Fairyland.

"Come on," said Kirsty. "Let's get back to Aunt Helen."

The girls ran all the way to the cookie department, hoping that the cookie machine would work now. When they reached the cookie design room, they found Aunt Helen coming out with a big smile on her face.

"Just in time, girls!" she said. "The engineers fixed the cookie machine, and I'm about to go and watch the first batches coming out!"

Feeling excited, the girls followed Aunt Helen to the main factory area. She pointed at a giant conveyor belt.

"Look," she said. "That's carrying the Chocolate Smiles into the oven!"

Rachel and Kirsty stood on their tiptoes and saw rows of happy chocolate chip faces going into the enormous oven.

"Now come around here," said Aunt Helen.

On the other side of the machine, another conveyor belt was carrying the first batch of baked cookies out of the oven.

"Jammy Hearts and Oaty Surprises!" said Rachel, clapping her hands together. "They look perfect."

"You can tell us if they taste perfect," said Aunt Helen.

She handed them each a cookie. As the girls took a bite, all the factory workers held their breath.

"DELICIOUS!" said Kirsty and Rachel together.

There was a loud

cheer from the factory workers, and Aunt
Helen grinned happily. She picked up
two boxes of cookies and handed them
to the girls.

"You can take
home the very
first boxes from
the assembly
line," she said.
"I hope you've
had a good
time today.
I've loved
showing you
around."

"It's been great," said Kirsty, giving her
aunt a big hug. "Thank you so much,
Aunt Helen. It was a fantastic birthday
present!"

"Let's save the cookies for your birthday tomorrow," Rachel suggested.

"Hopefully we can eat them to celebrate finding the other magic charms," said Kirsty in a low voice. "We still have two more to find. Do you think we can do it in time for Fairyland's Treat Day?"

"Definitely," said Rachel in a confident voice. She winked. "No matter how hard he tries, Jack Frost can't outsmart us—we have fairy magic on our side!"

THE SUGAR AND SPICE FAIRIES

Rachel and Kirsty found Lisa, Esme, Coco,
Clara, and Madeline's missing magic charms.
Now it's time for them to help

Layla
the Cotton Candy Fairy!

Join their next adventure in this
special sneak peek. . . .

Wheeeee!

Kirsty Tate smiled as she began climbing the steps up the giant slide with her best friend, Rachel Walker. Today she felt like the luckiest girl in the whole world! Not only was it her birthday, but she was at the Wetherbury Park Fair with Rachel—and the sun was beaming

down, too. Best of all, she and Rachel
were in the middle of another wonderful
magical fairy adventure. This time, they
were helping the Sugar and Spice Fairies!

"It's a long way up," Rachel
commented from behind Kirsty as they
climbed the steps. "We'll be able to see
for miles from the top."

"Yes," Kirsty agreed. Then she lowered
her voice. "We might even be able to see
a fairy from up there!" She crossed her
fingers hopefully at the thought. Meeting
another fairy would make her birthday
absolutely perfect!

It was spring break and so far it had
been a very exciting couple of days. At
the beginning of the week, Honey the
Candy Fairy had surprised them by
appearing in a pile of candy in Kirsty's

bedroom. She needed the girls' help to stop Jack Frost, who was up to his terrible tricks again. This time, he'd stolen the Sugar and Spice Fairies' magic charms! He was using them to help build himself an enormous Candy Castle.

The seven Sugar and Spice Fairies worked very hard to make sure that candy and treats in Fairyland and the human world tasted scrumptious. Without the fairies' magic charms, sweet things didn't taste good at all. Even worse, today was the annual Treat Day in Fairyland. The fairy king and queen wouldn't be able to give their traditional treat baskets to the other fairies unless all seven charms were safely returned.

Kirsty and Rachel had been helping the Sugar and Spice Fairies track down their magic charms. So far, they'd found five: the lollipop, cupcake, ice cream, cocoa bean, and cookie charms. Now there were just two fairies missing their charms — Layla the Cotton Candy Fairy and Nina the Birthday Cake Fairy. And with Kirsty's birthday party planned for that afternoon, she really hoped they could help both fairies before it was too late!

Just then, Kirsty reached the top of the steps and let out a gasp. "Wow!" she said. "You can see the whole fair from up here!"

Wetherbury Park was usually a quiet, calm place, full of dog-walkers and joggers, but today it was full of bustle and noise. It seemed like the whole village had come to the fair today!

"There's the teacup ride," Rachel said, pointing it out. "Oh, and the ball toss is right next to it."

"I can see my mom and dad!" Kirsty cried, waving excitedly. "Look, they're over by the cotton candy stand. I hope that means we can have some when we meet up with them."

"Ooh, yes," Rachel agreed. "And there's the mirror maze, I love those," she added. "But I don't see any fairies. Or goblins . . ."

RAINBOW magic ™

Which Magical Fairies Have You Met?

- ❑ The Rainbow Fairies
- ❑ The Weather Fairies
- ❑ The Jewel Fairies
- ❑ The Pet Fairies
- ❑ The Dance Fairies
- ❑ The Music Fairies
- ❑ The Sports Fairies
- ❑ The Party Fairies
- ❑ The Ocean Fairies
- ❑ The Night Fairies
- ❑ The Magical Animal Fairies
- ❑ The Princess Fairies
- ❑ The Superstar Fairies
- ❑ The Fashion Fairies
- ❑ The Sugar & Spice Fairies

■ SCHOLASTIC

Find all of your favorite fairy friends at
scholastic.com/rainbowmagic

HiT entertainment

RMFAIR